Dad's ship

A Harcourt Achieve Imprint

www.Rigby.com
1-800-531-5015

The ship is here.

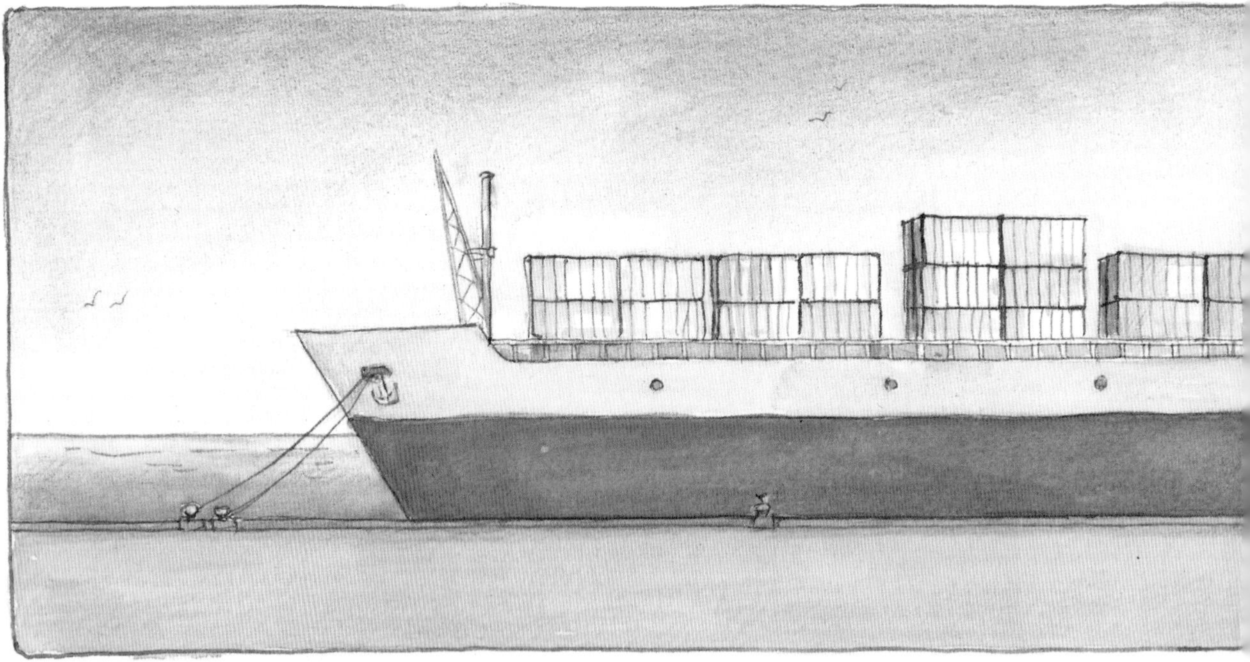

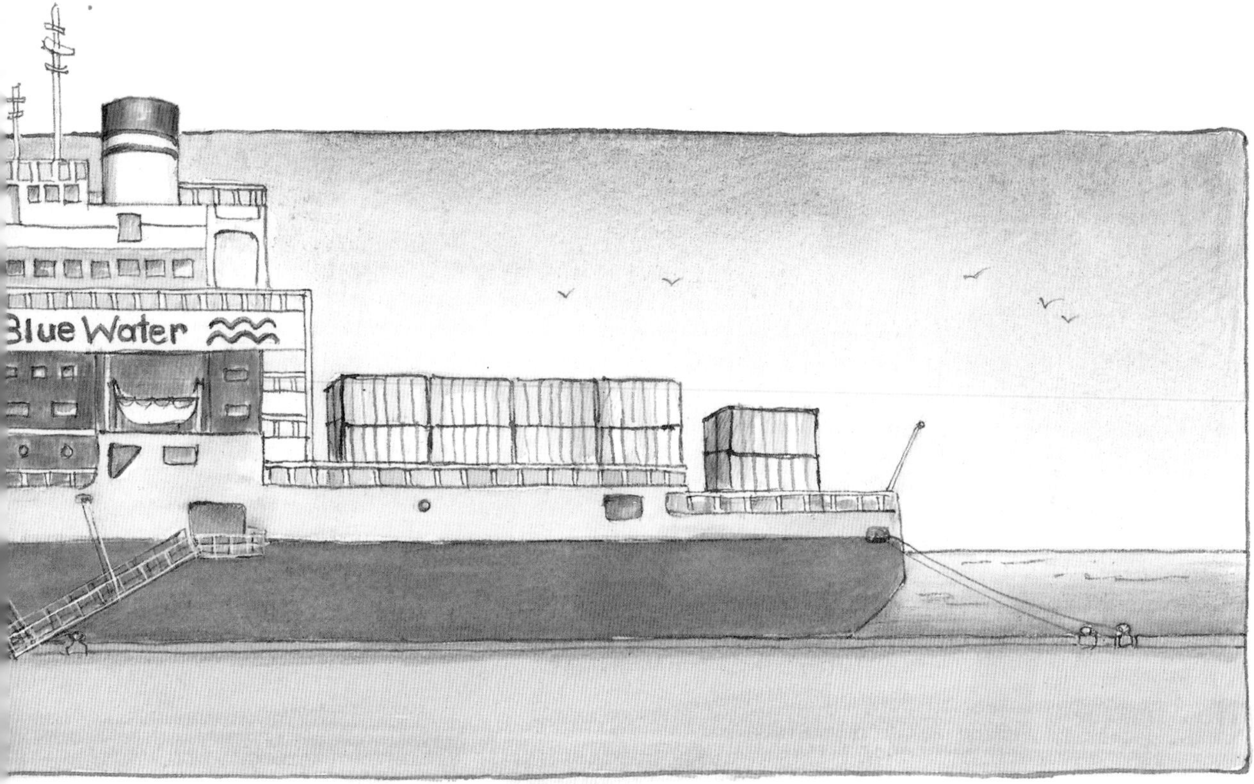
Blue Water

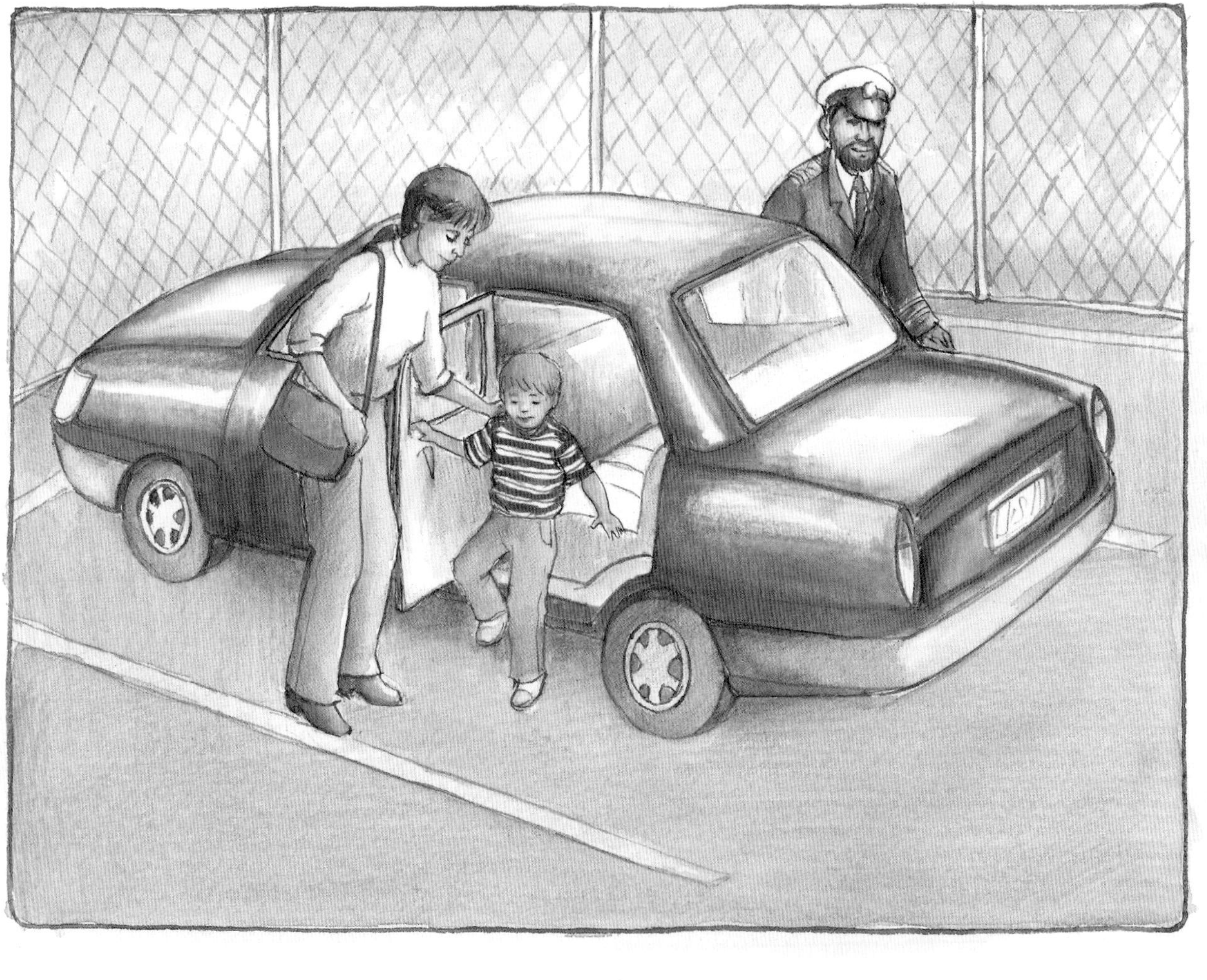

Dad is here.

Ben is here.

Mom is here.

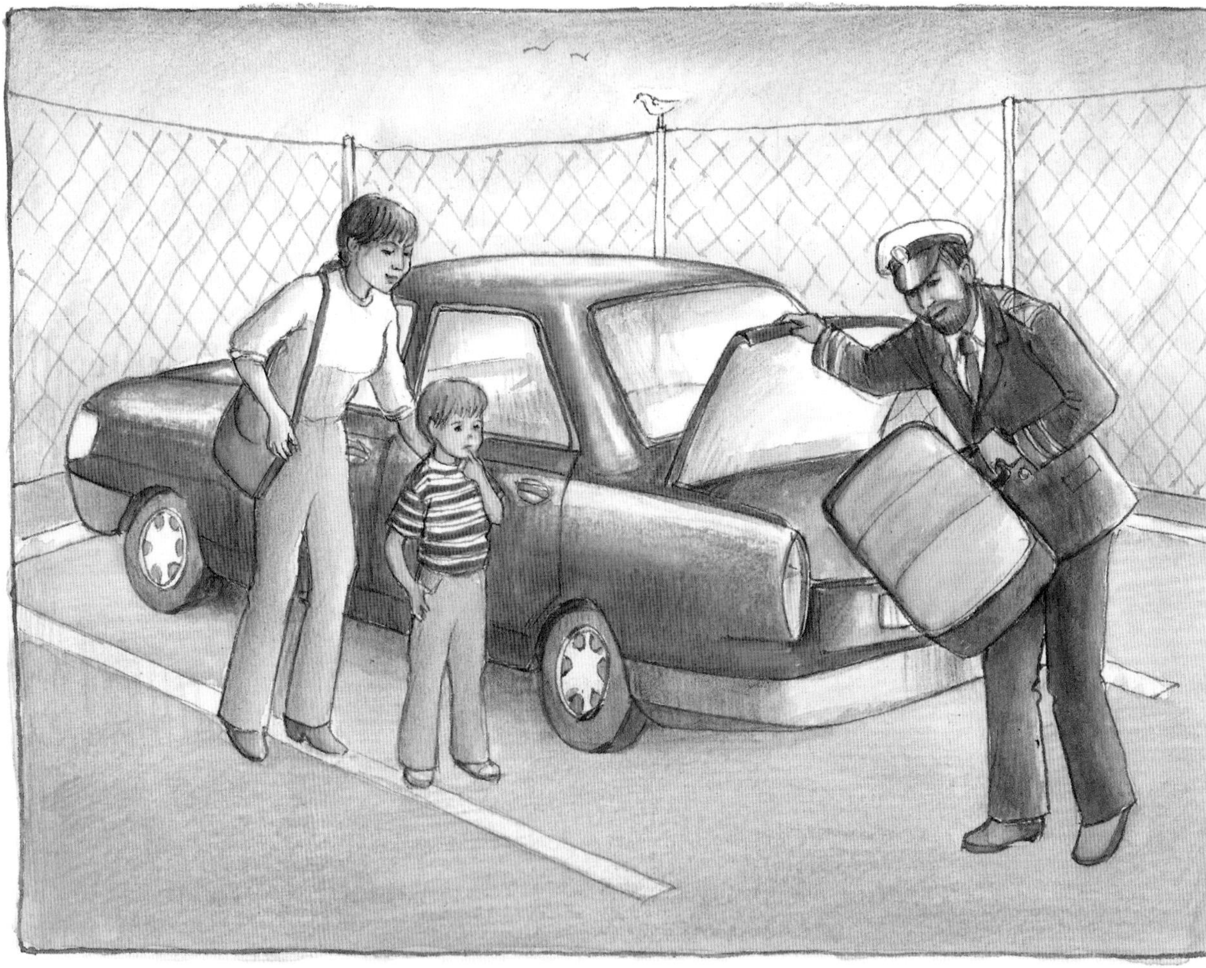

Here is Dad's bag.

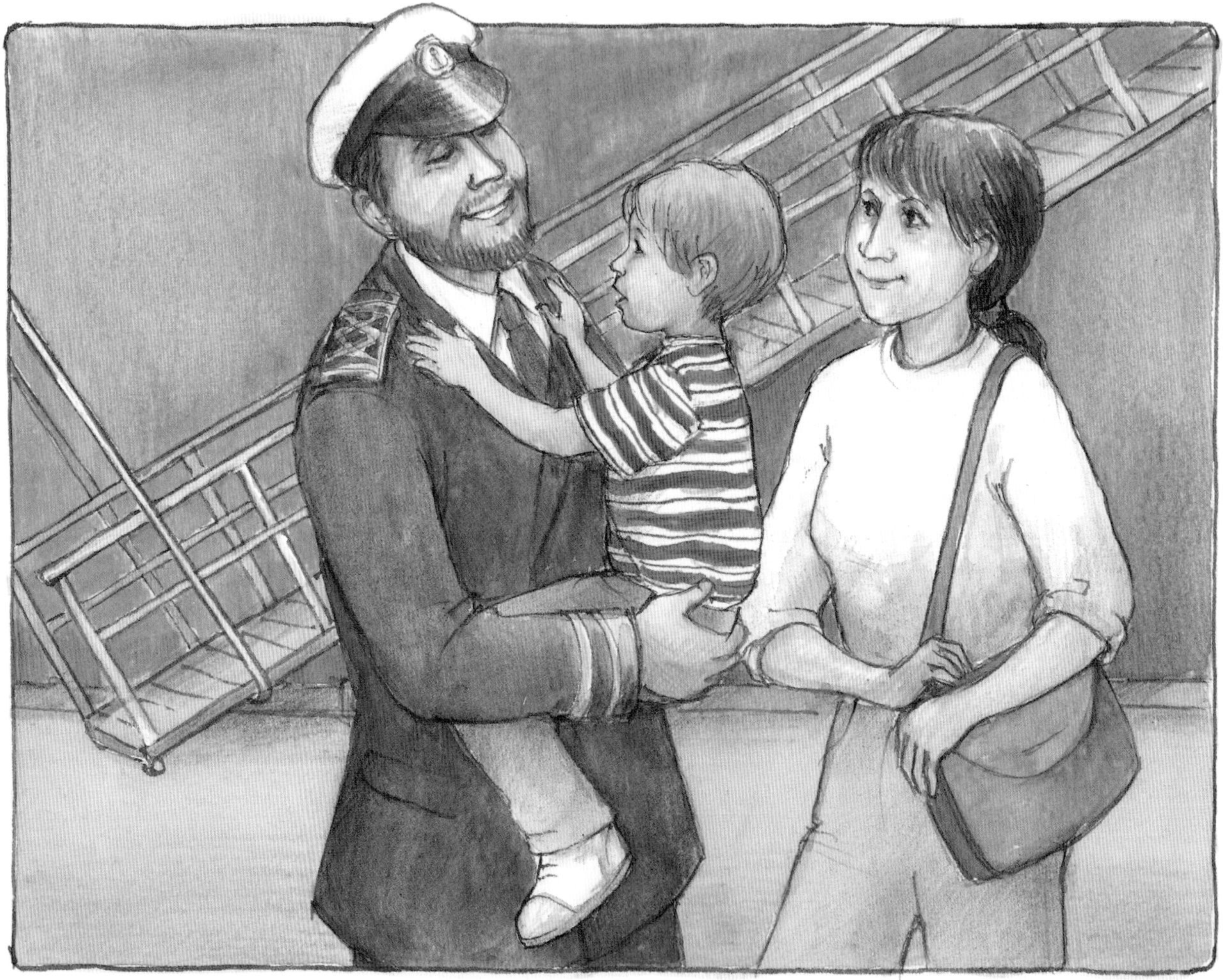

"Goodbye, Dad."

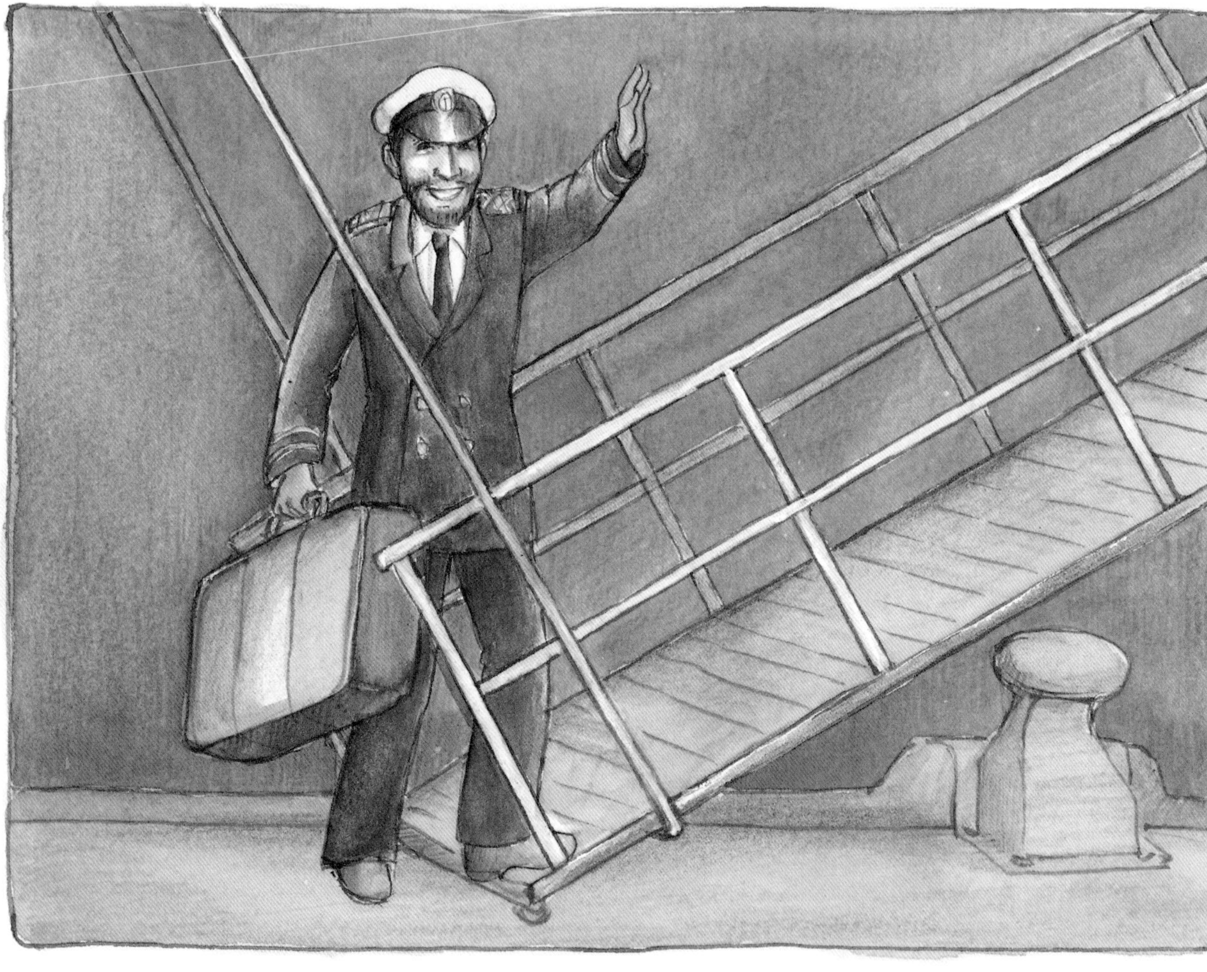

"Goodbye!"

11

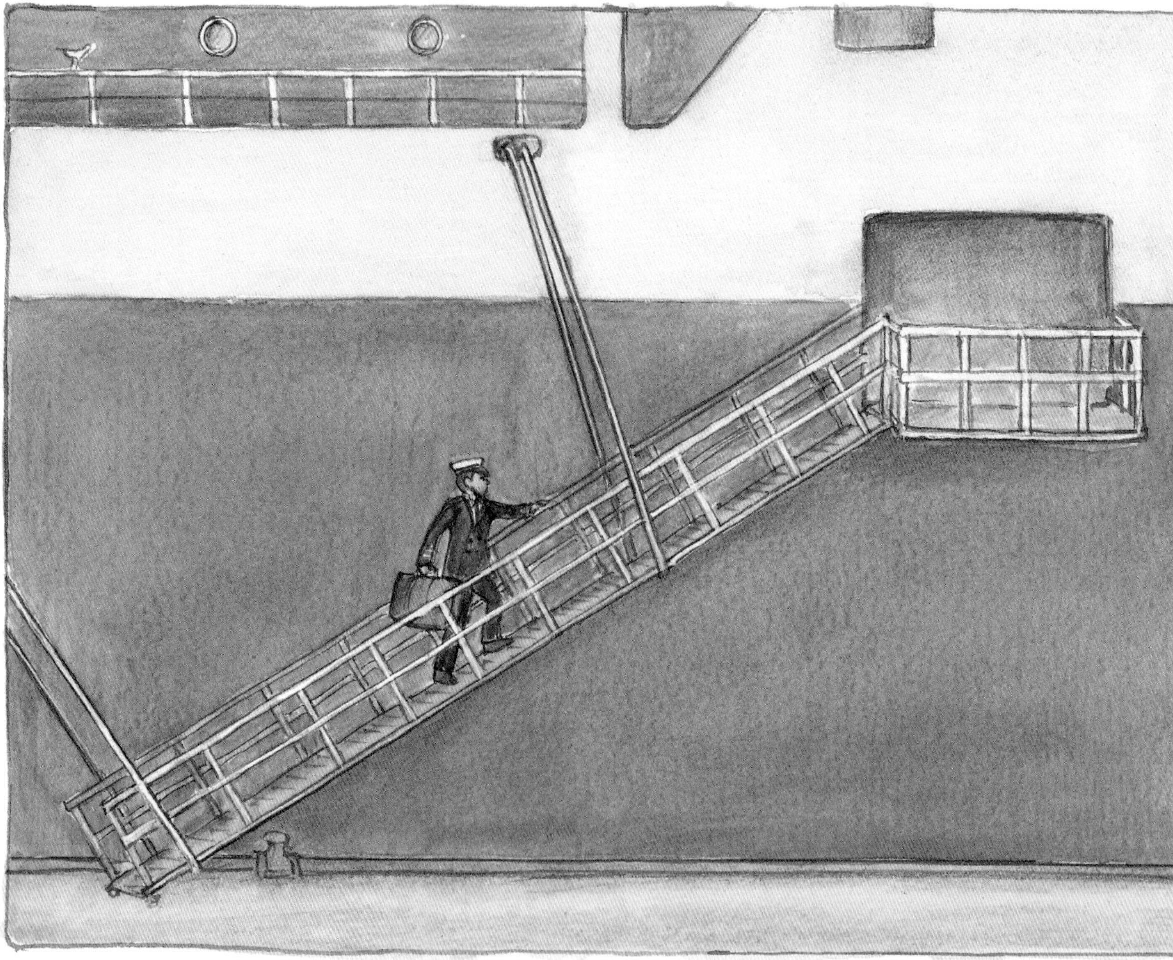

Dad is going

on the ship.

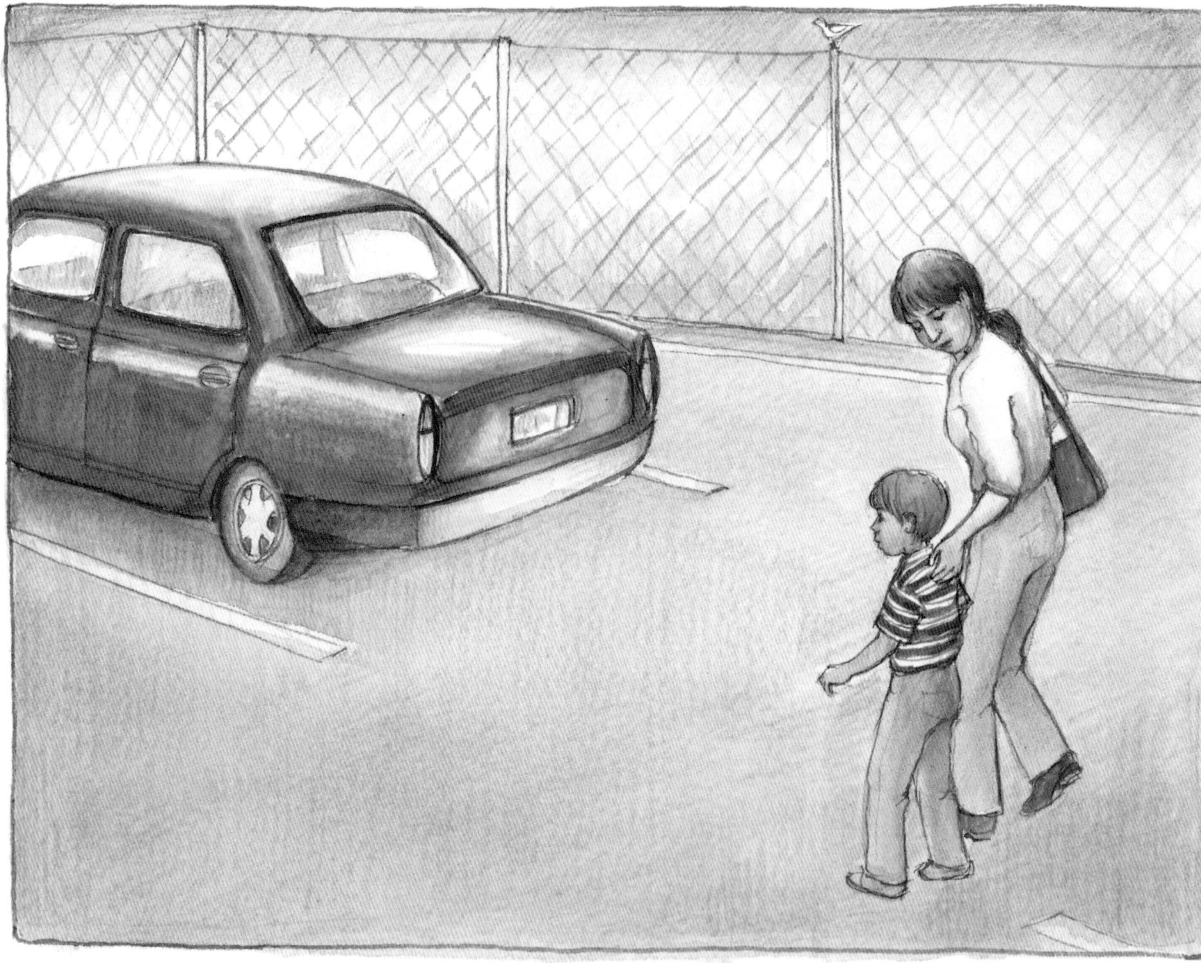

Mom is not going
on the ship.

Ben is not going
on the ship.

"Goodbye! Goodbye!"

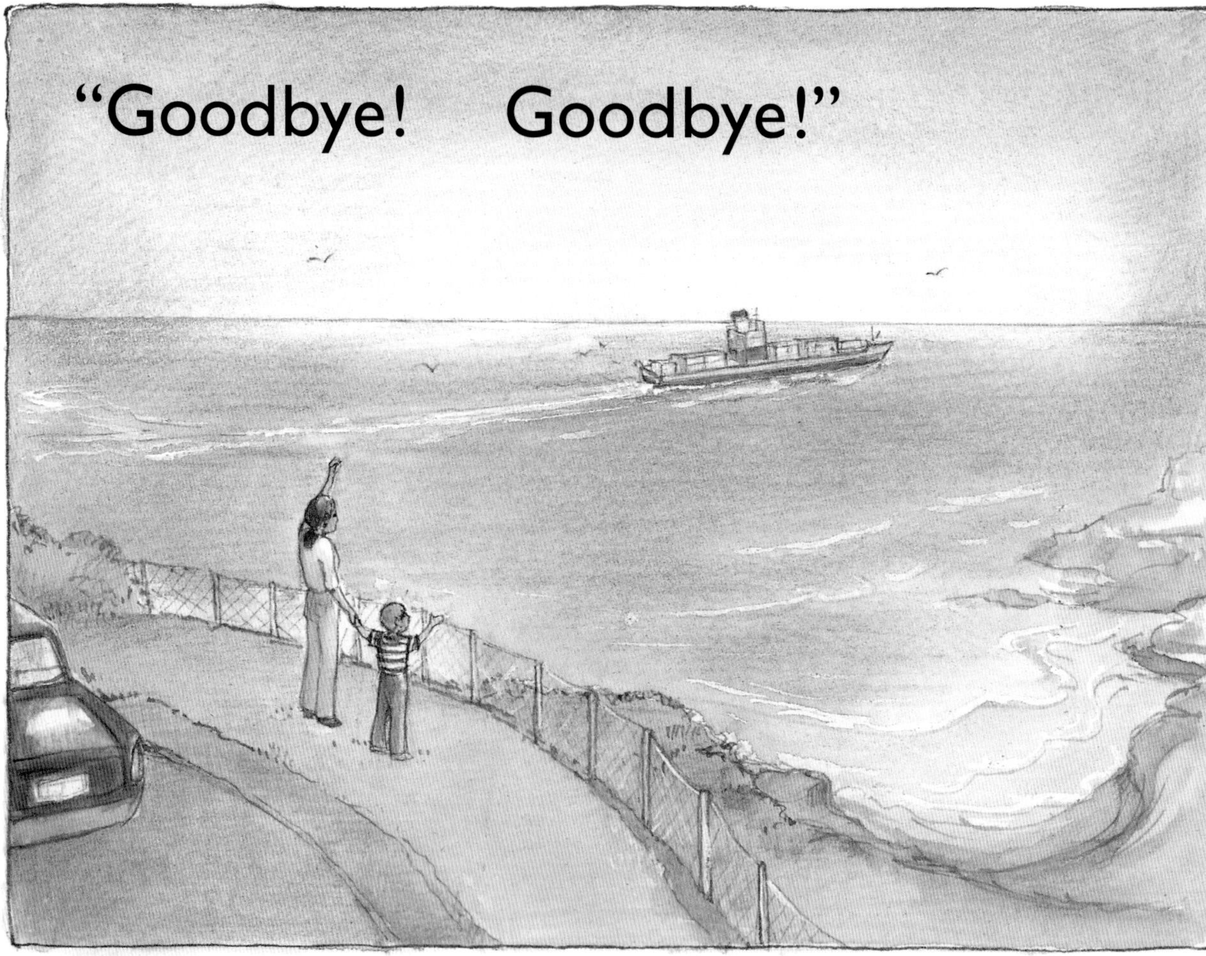